DEBACLE
IN
AUZRAERIA

CHARLES MWEWA

Published by:

ACP

Ottawa ON Canada

www.acpress.ca

ISBN: 978-1-998788-52-1

DEDICATION

For

Emmerance

CONTENTS

PROLOGUE

"And the LORD said unto Cain, where is Abel thy brother? And he said, I know not: Am I my brother's keeper?" (Genesis 4:9)

1 | KINGPENG

Gavo was excited.

He would be attending his sister's wedding in Kingpeng, a well renown resort in Auzraeria, a rich country in Central America.

He, and his sister, Belinda, last saw each other 25 years ago before she was adopted by Mr. and Ms. Kaleb when she was only 12 years old.

Gravo was 15 then.

Gravo grew up on the streets of Docrberg in Farisia and because of street smartness, he survived and owned a convenience store in Docrberg.

"Master, we need to diversify advertisements. Our competitors are going to social media," Beauty Pong, Gavo's longest serving cashier, suggested.

"Good idea, but which platform is good for business?" Gavo wanted more details.

"I think the likes of Facebook, 'X' or Twitter, and TikTok will do."

"Okay, create an account with Facebook just as a trial…"

"I will, now," Beauty said excitedly, without even letting Gavo finish his sentence.

Gavo was about to leave the shop when Beauty shouted.

"One more question, Master, how should I call the account?"

"Mhm…call it '*Cikaya Exclusives*,'" Gavo said.

"Just that…I mean, not your full name, 'Gavo Morrison Cikaya'?"

"Just that, not *my* name," Gavo said, with a sense of finality and he left.

***

Recently, Belinda and Gavo got hold of each other through Facebook.

But it was not easy.

Belinda recalled.

"Thank God you never changed your name, otherwise, I'd have thought that I lost my only brother forever," Belinda Kaleb had in-boxed Gavo.

"Yep, that's me, your bro – always Gavo Morrison Cikaya, never changed," Gavo had replied.

And that was the only reason why his sister found him on Facebook, because he went by the same name Gavo had used since they were little.

That, however, was not the same for Belinda.

When she was adopted, Belinda had become Belinda Kaleb.

Shortly after adopting her, Greg and Donelia Kaleb died.

They both died in a motorcycle accident in Bongoto, Auzraeria.

Belinda inherited a reclusive hacienda in the small town of Kingpeng, Auzraeria, estimated to be over US$190 million worth.

Belinda returned her real last name after the death of her adopted parents and went by the name of Belinda Kaleb Cikaya.

With the prudent management of the estate she inherited, Belinda became a very rich woman in a space of just about seven years.

On the eighth anniversary of Greg and Donelia Kaleb's passing, Belinda took her maidservant, Nye Borren, to their gravesite.

"Your departure was untimely, dearly beloved parents," Belinda began, "…but even to my own surprise, I have been a good manager of the estate you left me."

Nye handed a bouquet of white and red rose flowers and Belinda spread it on her parents' grave.

"Just before I leave," Belinda addressed her deceased parents again, "I should tell you that

I have created the very first social media account on Facebook, in fact, two, if I should add the one Nye had made for me last year at 'Exquisite Dating Enchantment,' where, hopefully, I may one day come and introduce my suitor from there."

Nye brought a leather jacket and covered her matron, and whispered, *"It's getting late, Ma'am, we better start off."*

***

It was the name "Cikaya" that prompted Belinda to send a friendly request and Gavo accepted.

When Belinda said "hi," Gavo never replied, because he did not check his Facebook account that often; Beauty did. But she never knew that Gavo had a sister.

From time to time, Gavo advertised some new merchandise he got at his profile, but he rarely checked anything else.

Belinda had become almost frustrated, because although Gavo had changed very much since they last saw each other, something in the inside told her that Gavo was the same brother she knew. She had canvassed

all over social media and that profile bearing the name "Cikaya" was the closest she got to her brother.

"Hope is never disappointed," Belinda had encouraged herself.

She had doubts, though, because Gavo put his location as Docrberg.
When she left, they lived in Harrisondale.

"But two people can't have the same name and live in the same country, well, it can happen, but what are the chances in 100?" Belinda contemplated.

Then she convinced herself, "Besides, they are of the same age, although they use 'Exclusives' to the name."

After many months of checking her Facebook for Gavo's response, she grew impatient, because there was none.
She decided to send him a bold message in all capitals:

"YOU MAY BE MY LONG-LOST BROTHER, GAVO MORRISON CIKAYA; I AM YOUR LONG-LOST SISTER,

BELINDA CIKAYA. RESPOND."

That, surely, arrested Gavo's attention. The very next day, after Beauty had brought that message to Gavo's attention, he replied.

"My *Sis*, I am him, your very own brother."

And as they say, the rest became history.

2 | HIGHJACKING

As the only brother, and now the only relative she had, Gavo would be the one who gave her away to Frank in marriage.

Belinda had sent Gavo an air ticket and made arrangements for his travel.

Gavo would arrive at least ten days before the wedding for rehearsals and preparations.

Frank would arrive five days before the wedding owing to the launch of his life-shaking invention of a Tickfogree Aierocar – a one-of-its-kind innovations.

The Tickfogree Aierocar, shortened for T.A was to be an airbus that literally could be

converted into a car. But it could only fly where it had been granted a permit.

While Frank had acquired land rights throughout Auzraeria, he would only acquire flight rights in certain parts of Auzraeria. He was granted flight rights from Bongoto, which was a nearby city to Kingpeng. Therefore, his itinerary included traveling to Auzraeria by his T.A and only fly to Kingpeng via Bongoto.

***

In Bongoto, Gavo's bus was highjacked by bandits at the middle of a mountainous side, in the middle of nowhere.

The bandits were demanding money and any valuables they could find on any passenger or in their bags.

They were also checking each passenger's passport, wanting to find a person who went by the name of "Frank Mantosha."

The bandits were dressed up as police officers when they staged a bogus roadblock.

"Get out of the bus!" The hijacking ringleader commanded.

He was holding a gun and pointing at the

driver.

Everyone was being searched up to their underpants.

Before his turn to be searched came, Gavo saw a *gentleman* stop in a state-of-the-art car on the pavement, asking, "Mr. Policeman. I am heading to Bongoto Airstrip. How do I proceed?"

GPS was not available in the mountainous side of the Archipelago.

Gavo got his chance.

As the ringleader was busily talking to Frank, as Gavo came to learn later, Gavo sneaked through the confusion and jumped into the back of T.A so that he could hide there and escape.

Before long, a disheveled, rough person made his way towards the special car holding Frank by his shirt collar and sleeves.

"This car is special, are you by chance called Frank, Frank Galando?" The ringleader asked.

"Y-e-s, Frank *Mantosha*?"

"You're *Mantosha*, Frank?" The ringleader

was confused.

"Y-e-s, Frank Mantosha, *Galando* is my social media nickname…but how did you know my name?"

"Well, you're an inventor, aren't you?" The ringleader asked, teasingly.

"You're right, I should have known the power of fame…"

As Frank was talking, the ringleader beckoned to the rest of his company as if saying to them, "We found him."

All the seven members of the ring squeezed themselves inside a five-seater plane-car.

"Drive," The ringleader ordered.

Frank started driving.
Both Frank and the bandits did not know that Gavo was in the hood of the car.
After driving for about 30 minutes, Belinda called.
Frank's phone was connected to the car.

The bandit boss commanded Frank, "Pick

it up. Talk. Don't say anything stupid or I will…"

The bandit was pointing a gun at Frank.

"I will be there shortly, Darling. I am trying to navigate some very inclement *weather* here," Frank said.

"But it is…" Belinda was interrupted.

"It only started raining a few minutes ago here…I will talk to you soon."

Hiding in the bonnet of the special car, Gavo heard some choking sound and he concluded that the gunman was trying to prevent Frank from talking.

Meanwhile, although Belinda could not dwell on it for long, she wondered why the *weather* could be "inclement" in Bongoto in summer.

But she decided to wait patiently for her husband-to-be.

Very soon, I will be Mrs. Galando, Belinda thought.

3 | MARIONKOBELL HOTEL

In the back, Gavo could barely hear the conversation because of strong winds. When they arrived near the airport, the car parked outside of a hotel, the Marionkobell Hotel, in Bongoto.

Gavo found a chance and escaped.

Since they don't know that I am in here, this is my chance, Gavo thought.

Gavo waited until the noise intensified in front of the car. He slowly removed his leg down the rear bumper, and then his left arm, holding firmly to the panel that lay astride the

wheel rims, and found a hole in the edges of the end-rims.

"*Finally, I am out*," he whispered to himself.

He ran as far as he could before he found some people and told them what was happening.

"Someone has been kidnapped by a bandit. You will find a burgundy luxury car parked at the back of the hotel. The man dressed in a khaki shorts and shirt is the one who has been kidnapped by the disheveled man."

But Gavo, being in a hurry, had forgotten to mention that the bandit was wearing a police uniform.

Gavo went to find a nearby pay phone so that he could call Belinda.

"Who is this?" Belinda answered the phone.

"It's me, Sis."

"Where are you, Brother?" Belinda asked.

"It's a long story. I only have my clothes on me; I have no money. We were attacked by bandits," Gavo explained.

"Attacked! Bandits!" Belinda shouted in disgust.

Belinda told Gavo to take a taxi all the way to Kingpeng.

"It will take ten or less hours, but don't worry, I will pay for it," she assured him.

***

"Officer, we were told that there was a kidnap going on in this car?" A guard was concerned.

"Here. No chance, I just escorted a suspect who was causing public nuisance in the area," answered the uniformed but disheveled police officer.

"Sorry, Officer. It was a false alarm."

"In my line of work, it happens all the time," remarked the disheveled police officer.

"Bye, Officer."

"Bye, sir."

***

"He's dying, Boss. I think he's revealed everything…"

"But he didn't give us the password to the vehicle. Muravi can't operate it beyond today. Ask him, beat him more. You hear me?"

"Yes, Boss."

Mikoshev left and when he reached the dungeon's torture chamber near Marionkobell Hotel, he took over the charge of torturing Frank.

The dungeons near the hotel had been abandoned by the City for a long time. And since they practically did not belong to anyone, the cartel had been hiding there since the massacre of 1000 villagers in the Auzraecress Region near Applecrest, the Capital City of Auzraeria.

The cartel itself had snatched the dungeons

from rival gangs and turned them into its own operation base.

Mikoshev inflicted the "death charm" technique on Frank. The technique was rarely used because the victim ended up deceased. It was only employed in extraordinary circumstances, and usually when the cartel did not desire to release the victim alive. The victim's anterior cingulate cortex-thalamus-insula area in the brain was pierced by a sharp, very long nail, causing sporadic pain and confusion.

"My…face, right thumb…" Frank struggled to breathe, then he went quiet.

"Remove the godforsaken needle…pour water on him…why did you do that at this time?" The Boss was furious at Mikoshev.

"We…have…" Mikoshev started.

"You did what, remember we only have his financial information and we need his family identity and how to operate his vehicle!"

"I know, Boss… but he revealed the truth…" Mikoshev defended himself. He knew

how spontaneous his boss could be. He was known to kill members of his own group.

"… his face…his right thumb… he said, Boss."

When Muravi tried it, it worked. The face followed by the right thumb started the vehicle, opened the safe in the vehicle and the laptop in the safe.

"We got it, Boss!" Sharon, one of the cartel members exclaimed with joy. She had discovered a stash of UAS dollars in the safe. She was the one the Boss trusted to keep the cartel funds.

In their newly found excitement, they had forgotten about the dying Frank. When they checked on him, he was already dead.

"What do we do next, we can't be taking a cadaver with us. It will soon begin to decompose."

"But…Boss… there is a fridge in the vehicle," Drew Fo, one of the group members suggested.

"But that fridge is very small," Honda counteracted.

"I have an idea…" Mikoshev did not wait to explain his idea first. He left for the kitchen and brought a knife. He chopped off both Frank's head and right thumb and returned, "… problem solved," he announced.

Although the boss was furious because Mikoshev did not wait to get clear instructions, but the boss could not deny that Mikoshev's actions had solved their problem.

"Your punishment for not discussing the option with me is to make this body disappear without a trace, you hear me, Miko?"

"Yes, Boss, I do."

Drew Fo and Sharon hastened to dishevel their boss so that he should "look exactly like Frank."

"Wow, you guys are magicians… now I can have both the bucks and the Beauty…let the glory begin!"

Within hours, the cartel was planning to be on its way to the resort town of Kingpeng.

***

"Bye, Sweetie, I just arrived at the hotel and I will see you in the morning," George Garland, a pilot, told his wife.

George and Feliciano just returned from their honeymoon in the UAS where they had spent two weeks in the resort town of Myrtle Beach. Since they returned, that was his fourth day on the job and he was already assigned to a local schedule flying customers from Applecrest to Bongoto. He lived in Applecrest.

George finished talking on the phone with his wife and he was about to slot his iPhone 16 in his right pilot uniform when he heard the click of a gun on his right ear lobe.

"Stay right there, don't move or…"

George immediately knew what was happening. The man in a police uniform was already directing him towards a luxurious

burgundy car parked by the entrance of Marionkobell Hotel, just a good distance away from CCTV. George had a gun barrel pointed at his belt by a "policeman" walking and talking calmly behind him. No one suspected any fowl play.

"Here, get in," a man the pilot later came to know as Mikoshev commanded him.

Inside the vehicle another man greeted him and told him to feel at home.

"I am just borrowing you to fly this machine to Kingpeng, that's all," the man whom George later came to know as "the Boss," instructed him.

"B-u-t…" George stammered.

"But what…you want to live and see your wife or fly this thing and return home safely?" Mikoshev threatened.

"Miko, I am the one talking here…" The Boss warned.

"Sorry, Boss," Mikoshev apologized.

"Okay, can you fly this or not…"

Before the boss could complete his sentence, Sharon threw a manual on George's laps.

"*Incredible*," George spoke to himself after perusing through the manual.

"What did you say?" Drew Fo asked.

"This is an incredible machine, are you sure you are going to free me if I fly it for you?" The question was being directed at the boss, so no one answered. Then the boss responded in a matter of factly manner.

"Oh, yes, George," the boss replied looking at the displayed name tag on George's pilot uniform.

George was eager to try the machine. He pressed a combination of buttons from the manual and the wings began to populate.

"Not here, son of a gun," Sharon was upset.

"Hey, *Nunu*, don't be disrespectful to the one who takes you on their wings," the boss rebuked Sharon.

"Sorry about that, Captain, but she *is* right; you can't fly it on the regular road. Let's go to Bongoto Airfield, here is the clearance."

***

"We've arrived, sir. This was the greatest joyride of my life," George was all over the machine.

"You like it? By the way, my name is Frank, I am the patent holder of this machine; my pilot became ill suddenly. If you stay, I can hire you on a good pay?"

"I…I…" George was indecisive.

"What, didn't you just say that you liked it?" Frank was getting upset.

"Oh, no, no, Boss, it's not like that…remember I said that I have a wife, sir…"

"…and you want to go to her…alright…Miko escort our friend *home*…" Frank ordered.

Mikoshev and George left. George was saying something to Mikoshev but it was not audible. But George kept looking back and pointing in the opposite direction.

After about 30 minutes, Mikoshev returned alone. He had dirt all over his hands and there was a small red spot on his brows.

"Done, Boss, he's *home*," Mikoshev reported.

"Alright, let's now drive to Sweet Belinda's ranch," Frank ordered.

4 | "FRANK"

"Your brother is suffering from PTSD," informed Dr. Beze, when Brenda asked why Gavo was wringing and uttering meaningless words in his hospital bed.

When he arrived in a taxi, an eight-hour ride, Gavo was extremely exhausted. Belinda had called her private physician and explained the situation. Dr. Beze recommended that they brought in Gavo to his private hospital immediately. When they arrived, Dr. Beze confirmed what she had suspected.

"If you did not bring him in earlier than now, he would have relapsed," she said.

"Thank you, Doc.; what happens next?" Belinda asked.

"He must be fine in a couple of days. For now, he will stay in his hospital bed for observation."

"Sure, no problem," Belinda sighed.

Gavo was put on observation. And because he was showing signs of dehydration, he was connected to an IV tube to receive intravenous fluids.

Belinda gave Moffat, one of her trusted male servants, charge to assist a Personal Support Worker (PSW) assigned to attend to Gavo.

***

Two days after Gavo was hospitalized, "Frank" arrived at the hacienda in style, driving the T.A and he arrived at Belinda's ranch.

"Your moustache looks exactly as in the photos, except I pictured you to be much shorter than this," Belinda said as she hugged "Frank" while exploring his special vehicle.

"This is truly state-of-the art," exclaimed a maidservant who was assisting Belinda to welcome "Frank."

Holding Belinda tightly in his huge arms, "Frank," said, "You're exactly as I imagined, only more beautiful in person."

Belinda was flattered.
She could not hide her feelings.
She sobbed for couple seconds while resting her long neck on his broad shoulders.
Indeed, Frank and Belinda had exchanged many photos of each other. Although they had never met in person till that day, they had established a deeper connection and were, virtually, very comfortable with each other.

"I am sorry that you had to experience such bad weather on your way here," Belinda regretted.

"I am fine, Darling," the man who was still

holding Belinda tightly, assured.

After they let go of each other, "Frank" suggested that he needed some time to himself to recuperate from the tumultuous trip.

"Surely, it makes sense. Your cottage is ready and there are servants there to attend to your every detail," Belinda comforted.

"For that, I don't want you to worry. I'll have my entourage attend to me when they arrive in the next 24 hours. I sent them to do an errand for me, us, you know – it's a wedding surprise," the man bantered.

"I love *surprises*," Belinda said.

"I know, and you'll have plenty of *that* from me," the man exhaled.

"My brother…" Belinda started, just as they were about to leave each other's company.

"Yes…" the man turned gracefully, "What about *your* brother?"

"He arrived; he's here, I mean. He also had a rough journey over in *Bongoto*, but he's recuperated."

"What happened to him?" 'Frank' wanted to know.

"I won't bother you with that; he's here, that's what matters. Go on and be ready for dinner hosted in your honor tonight," Belinda disclosed.

They parted ways, momentarily.

***

Gavo was truly confused.

"Frank" spoke like one of the bandits, in fact, the ringleader, but he looked like the hijacked man.

The bandit had detained Frank and got all the information he could about everything Frank was and did. The bandit had killed Frank but nobody knew.

"Frank" was avoiding getting intimate with Belinda, feigning, "As a holy man, we will only

have intimacy after we are pronounced husband and wife. Meanwhile, to avoid committing sin, I will be as much distant from you in the guestroom as possible."

People sound more differently when they are in-person than on the phone. We spent two years speaking on the phone and still I can't recognize that voice I fell in love with, but he's modest and he has morality, Berlinda thought.

"Thank you for being protective, Darling," Belinda said.

"Any time," 'Frank' responded.

***

The day of special dowry came. And "Frank's" comrades who would be on the line-up had arrived.
But Gavo was mystified.

"That's the man who pointed a gun at me," Gavo recalled, "…and that is the person who told us to get out of the bus."

But those men and woman came in suites

and driving nice cars. They did not look like bandits at all.

Gavo tried to converse with her sister, but she was all over the moon and very busy.

***

"Boss, the hacienda is truly magnificent. It could be worth as much as over UAS$120 million," Sharon reported.

The boss was not paying attention; he was busily cleaning his Beretta M9 pistol.

"Boss, *Nunu* is talking to you," informed Mikoshev.

"I have heard… but there's something troubling me, Gavo…who's this guy?"

"I looked into him. He's subtle as he's street savvy. I hear that he's a conman. He could be here for the same reason as us…" Honda commented.

"What do you mean, Boss, command me to eliminate him?" Mikoshev suggested.

All the seven members of the cartel nodded their heads in agreement, but the Boss overruled them.

"I don't think so. I think he's her true brother. But I would suggest that we plant seeds of doubt in Belinda to buy some time…"

There was murmuring going on and five of them said, "Boss is right," but Honda kept silent.

"Are you with us, Boy?" Sharon asked, directing her question to Honda.

But Honda did not respond to Sharon, he directed his question to his father.

"Dad, remember the Maskevial Case?"

When all the members of the cartel were wondering what the Maskevial Case was, the boss was walking steadily toward his son, hugged him and said, "Don't worry, Son, I have got this one tight."

The father and son remained in the hugging posture for close to a minute. Tears rolled

down each other's cheeks as they silently remembered a fatal heist that went terribly wrong.

Honda had just turned seventeen. Medea Antiviap Paul, the boss' deceased wife, had suggested robbing a nearby credit union, the Maskevial Bank.

"I would rather we did it today," Medea had suggested, "I pass over there every day and I have studied the place very well."

"But, Sweetheart, Honda and I need some time to also understand what you know; we're a team, remember?"

Medea had been too overconfident. She ignored clear advice and she thought that she was ready.

On November Third, she decided to go solo, without involving her husband and son.

I will surprise them with a stash of money when I return from robbing that bank, she thought, excitedly.

That evening, the boss and his son were called to identify a body. It was Medea Paul. She had successfully robbed the bank of UAS$1.8 million but lack of preparation cost her life.

News reports that evening said that the security guard at the Maskevial branch had been authorized to carry a gun. The branch had been susceptible to robberies in the past and the credit union was the only lending agency in the area. Neighbors had petitioned the mayor to exempt that branch to equip its security guards to carry live ammunition and to fire and kill if necessary.

But Medea and her family were newer in that area and they were not aware of the bylaw.

Since then, when they lost Medea to a single bullet in her back, the boss had promised his son to honor the memory of his mother by creating "the most effective, efficient but ruthless money-stealing team in Auzraeria."

The gang became known as the Antiviap Cartel, in honor of Medea. When they reported her death in the media, the police did not have

any clues as to Medea's middle name or Antiviap. And over seven years, no one had been able to figure out the significance of the name Antiviap or how the cartel acquired it.

After the Maskevial incident, the very first recruit father and son added to the group was Muravi Mushitou, a born computer genius. He never went to any formal school but as early as two years old, he was "addicted" to computer games. Childhood friends of his praised him as having "pure instincts; he never lost a game."

One day, Muravi won a computer baiting anonymity contest for UAS$20,000.00 but the organizers refused to give it to him. After investigation, they had concluded that "he's a street boy of no fixed aboard, therefore, no one will come claiming his reward. With his computer skills, Muravi had dug out all the credentials and whereabouts of the organization.

And he approached a rusty but tough guy in his neighborhood called Mikoshev Vodhab. At eight years of age, he went to a juvenile detention facility for stealing his neighbor's Apollo Pro motorized scooter, and since then,

he had been in and out of prison.

Mikoshev went on a slaughter of all the three masterminds of the anonymity award contest and he recovered Muravi's reward. Since then, the two were inseparable.

So, when he was recruited, Muravi suggested to the father and son to give Mikoshev a chance, "He'll do all the dirty work for you, Boss."

Their first heist was flawless.

Muravi had hacked into the Lottery Bank's servers and had disabled access to the facility and the alarm system.

"You! Pack the money into that sack," Mikoshev had commanded a beautiful blonde teller of about 22 years.

"But the till machines have all malfunctioned; they can't open. We have been trying all morning to open them to no avail," she said.

Then the one they referred to as the "Boss," ordered, "Mura, do the trick," and he did. He temporarily enabled the system on his laptop.

All the till machines opened.

"Oh, wow!" Sharon, as the beautiful bank teller came to be known, exclaimed.

Sharon "Mosquito" Nunibel (*Nunu*) begged the Boss to join the cartel. And she had been in charge of the group's financial affairs ever since.

During the "Inbovia Convenience" break in, the group had lost the key to a stolen gateway car.

When they were being pursued on foot, "Mosquito" pretended to be a pregnant woman.

She got into a taxi and then put a gun to Drew Fo's head. She directed him to drive in the direction of the robbery gone wrong.

Drew Fo cornered the police and got all the four group members into the taxi and they made the escape.

From then, Drew Fo, a very savvy taxi driver, had joined the cartel as its chief driver and mechanic.

***

"We need to get this one right. This could be our last project before we retire in luxury," 'Frank,' the boss, recommended.

They were discussing business very late at night when everyone at the ranch was very fast asleep.

"Then what do we do with this Gavo guy?" Sharon asked.

"Leave him to me, *Nunu*. You all know that nobody plays poker on me," 'Frank' said.

Everyone nodded their heads in agreement.

5 | PROVIDENCE

Gavo, finally, had a chance to talk to "Frank." But Gavo had no idea that "Frank" was plotting to terminate him.

All I wants is to be pronounced husband and wife so that I can finally have access to all the fortunes of Belinda, 'Frank' thought.

It was a very clear and sunny Saturday morning in Kingpeng. Gavo got closer to "Frank" at breakfast prepared by Nye.

Gavo would have almost believed that that was a true Frank. But due to sheer luck or

Providence, "Frank" received a call.

"Hello, *Nunu*, what's up?"

"You forgot to leave instructions today, what do we do?"

"Frank" put his right hand on the cellphone and said, "Excuse me, Gavo, I must take this one."

Gavo pretended to be disinterested in what was being discussed.

"Go and talk, don't mind me," Gavo said.

"Frank" did not go very far, and he spoke to Sharon.

"Don't let anyone open the refrigerator in the T.A…"

"What if Belinda comes and asks us to open it, Sir?"

"Not even Belinda, especially, as you know, our lifeline is in there."

When "Frank" returned to continue breakfast with Gavo, Gavo pretended like everything was just like "Frank" left them.

Slowly, Gavo earned "Frank's" trust and they spent some of their free time driving the T.A around the hacienda.

When "Frank" left the T.A briefly, to attend to the call of nature, Gavo quickly opened the refrigerator and what he saw in the box there, almost made him puke.

There was a chopped off finger of a human being.

When "Frank" returned, Gavo pretended as if nothing had happened.

Gavo was wondering why "Frank" had a human finger in the car's refrigerator. His mistrust of "Frank" even grew more.

This brat marrying my sister, no way. He looks like a murderer, Gavo thought.

Then "Frank" made a suggestion.

"Brother-in-law?" 'Frank' asked.

"I am here, Brother."

"My guys will not be here today until

tomorrow morning. I have sent them to run some errands. I need you to get us some bottles of gin in downtown, can you assist me?" 'Frank' asked.

"Of course, Brother," Gavo agreed.

Then Gavo watched "Frank" open the refrigerator and taking out the box there, he went to the rear side of the T.A and came back with some dollars.

I know what is happening. This guy is nasty; he is using the finger to open the safe, Gavo thought.

And to his confirmation. Gavo heard an automated message after "Frank" had left the rear of the car. And the automated message said: "Success. Lock on."

Gavo left for downtown.

***

This unknown person has been calling me for a while, I am not picking up. Last time I did, they almost store my identity, Beauty thought.

Gavo was getting desperate. All he had was few dollars to make an international call. He had left his cellphone at the hacienda.

He walked to an intercity Internet café and asked if they offered a texting service.

"We don't do it here, but we have email service," a café owner said.

Gavo had to think fast.

"Okay, let me email, no, let me send a message through Facebook, I just saw on the poster that you offer that service here?"

"Sure," the café owner offered Gavo a free computer and login code.

"It worked, how much do I owe you?" Gavo asked.

"You will pay after use; it's UAS$4.00 per hour."

Gavo thought to himself, *That imposter gave me UAS$100.00; I do have some change.*

The problem was to remember the

password to their Facebook account. Gavo had forgotten or he never even asked what password she used. But he quickly remembered the name he had suggested to Beauty.

"*I think I said 'Cikaya Exclusives,'*" Gavo recalled.

After just one search, there it was and there was a conversation going on their Facebook profile. Beauty was explaining to one of the followers about the availability of some type of oriental food spices.

Gravo tried to comment but he could not. He tried to "inbox," Beauty, but he still could not.

"Hey, I need your help here," Gavo waved at the owner of the café.

Fortunately, the café was not very busy that time of the day, just past noon; many people were having lunch.

After explaining his situation, the café owner suggested that he should open a separate account and then "like" or "follow" the "Cikaya Exclusives" account.

It worked.

Gavo could both inbox and "outbox" Beauty.

The message he sent read, "I AM THE ONE CALLING NONSTOP. PLEASE PICK UP. GAVO!"

Fortunately, Beauty saw the message.

***

Gavo was eager to return to the hacienda where he had left his cellphone locked in his suitcase. Initially, he had not intended to use it. He was supposed to attend the wedding and quickly return to Docrberg, Farisia, to run his business.

But "Frank" changed everything and Gavo was prepared to protect his sister at all costs.

After all, she's my only family now. If I tank in business, it doesn't matter as long as Belinda is safe, Gavo thought.

When he arrived at the hacienda in a taxi, he rushed to his bag and got his phone but it was out of charge.

"It's dead. It might take longer to charge so I can get the answers to the questions I gave Beauty to research," Gavo spoke to himself.

That evening, Gavo pretended to be nice to "Frank" and they even had some drinks together.

But in the inside, he was itching to know what Beauty found about "Frank Galando," and the "T.A."

When he returned to his room that night, his cellphone was fully charged.

This is what I found: Indeed, there is a person called Frank Mantosha here who is a very rich man and who invented a T.A which can both double as a car and as an airplane. It uses something called aeronautic technology or something like that, some sort of, it can *think* by itself.

Yes, as you asked it has a refrigeration system on board, a disposable washroom and it can be turned into a recreational vehicle or an RV, but that technology is developing and will go into the next set of T.A's to be released next year.

There's one thing that caught my attention, though, this guy seems to have two names that he uses in different fora. On his website, he uses 'Frank K. Mantosha,' but online and

on social media, he uses 'Frank Galando.' I am confused, because that photo I have just sent you, is on both of his profiles.

Master, is he your sister's fiancé, well, you are truly lucky…

Beauty.

Gavo began to analyze the photo and information that he had received from Beauty via the text.

"Of course, this is the photo of true Frank when he was a bit younger. The haircut is the same, so is the moustache. But the eyes are patently different. The Frank in the photo has brown, large eyes, they can't be missed… but this imposter has bluish small eyes, has Belinda also missed this one? How about his physique, I heard her say that he expected Frank to be a bit shorter, but this guy is by my estimation about 5.8 feet? Are we missing something here?

"When they went into the T.A, there was only one person, one Frank in there, how come six more people joined him, and what are the chances in one trillion that the same number of the bus hijackers just happened to be the same number of these thugs… I can't let this go

*unchallenged…although my sister is madly in
love and can't understand reason…"*

That night, Gavo had a hard time sleeping.
He kept tossing the whole night.

Then before a deep sleep fell upon him, he
reenacted the day in his mind:

> *I went to an Internet café there and googled
> the T.A and what I found shocked me, but
> Beauty's revelations have shocked me even
> more. Exactly as I had thought, the T.A has
> a safe in the rear which uses finger-recognition
> technology to open. Oh…ho…mhm…I get it
> now…*
>
> *Now I know what happened. This
> swindler kidnapped Frank and forced him to
> reveal everything and then he murdered him,
> carrying off his finger to help in opening the
> safe. He then studied everything he could about
> Frank, impersonated him and came pretending
> to be him. But wait, how did he manage to
> know so much about Frank?*

That last question troubled Gavo.

"I will not do anything stupid until I find more

proof," Gavo whispered to himself.

6 | LAPTOP

"Sis, it's a good, to day spending this bright morning introducing your fiancé to the hacienda, what do you think?" Gavo lobbied his sister.

Before she could respond, Gavo offered her a bottle of champagne he had bought the previous day.

"Here, take it with you, have fun the two of you."

He's exactly the same. He once tricked me into dating Garrimond Charles by offering me candy.

Anyway, that's what I missed the most about him, Belinda thought as she simultaneously received the bottle and said, "Thank you, Bro."

His group was still away; they would be returning in an hour's time. So, "Frank" found it both romantic and convenience to spend some time inspecting the hacienda.

Afterall, all this shall be mine, "Frank" thought.

"Frank" went out for a routine walk with Belinda around the hacienda. Gavo took advantage.

"This is the only time I have, before his minions return later this afternoon. Let's see what this robber has," Gavo said, albeit inaudibly.

Gavo went to the servant quarters "Frank" occupied and searched everything he could lay his eyes on.

Luckily, he found a laptop hidden under a pile of clothes.

It had the name "Frank K. Mantosha" written on it.

When he turned on the power button,

immediately a notice came up, "Swipe your finger."

Gavo was shocked.

I get it. This robber got all the information about Frank from his laptop. He can open it with the finger, he thought.

Gavo would have wanted to have access to the finger but it was inside the T.A refrigerator and "Frank" had the keys. But he had had enough information to know what was going on. It was now time to come up with a plan to rescue his sister.

"These guys are dangerous. Any mistake here might cost not only my life but also that of my sister," Gavo talked to himself.

Gavo had come up with three ways of rescuing his sister.

First, I would talk to my sister and warn her that the guy she is intending to marry is not her Frank but a murderer. But the problem with this option is that it would be too emotional for Belinda and will she even believe

that her real Frank is, actually, dead? And if that becomes the case, where would I find that evidence? Of course, "Frank" will deny that there is a finger in the refrigerator.

Gavo reasoned that the first option was dead on arrival. Then he thought of another option.

What if I steal the finger, the cellphone and the laptop from "Frank", open them and show Belinda? But the problem with this idea is that it will prove nothing to Belinda. The finger will be a great piece of evidence that Frank is dead, no doubt, but has Belinda even seen Frank's finger in reality? And who would be the better culprit than the guy who has his finger, except that he can say anything to exculpate himself? And besides, Belinda may end up accusing me of murdering her fiancé or worse.

Gavo reasoned that the second option did not sit well with him, too.

Then he came up with a third option. It sounded better in his mind.

I will stage a kidnap of my own sister. That way the son of a bat, "Frank," will not suspect Belinda and will leave Belinda alone. I can always redeem myself with the truth later. This will both buy time and delay or permanently cancel the wedding.

That thought pleased Gavo. He was ready to risk everything to be his sister's keeper.

7 | IMPASSE

Margaret Westburn approached Officer Sullivan, and said, "Sir, the Chief of Police wants a word with you."

It was Tuesday, and the weather was soggy in most of Auzraeria, including in the Kingpeng-Bongoto region. Officer Sullivan was a huge tower of a man, six-feet tall, weighing around 350 pounds.

"Sure, Maggy, is there anything the matter, something I should know?"

"Nothing related to you personally, I think

it is related to the kidnapping incident in Kingpeng."

When he reached the Chief of Police's office, a smaller man, of about fifty-two years greeted him with a glass of ginger ale, "You want some?"

"Sure, Sir…I am thirsty…"

"…as you may have heard, there is a ruckus happing in Kingpeng. A man who claims to be a brother to the lady he's holding hostage just lost it and went on rampage. He believes that his brother-in-law to-be is an imposter…" the Chief of Police, needed not finish his sentence, he flipped a few pages among hundreds lying unorganized on his desk, and found it –

"Aha…here it is," he threw some pieces of paper on Officer Sullivan.

"Thank you, Sir, I will be on it straightaway."

"Send me intermittent reports, use my secretary."

"Yes, Sir, Ms. Westburn has always been efficient."

His name was Moses "Sweetness" M'bogma, nicknamed so, because he was ever imbibing something sweet all the time. He was the youngest, at 45 years of age, when he got appointed to the Chief of Police office. Rumors had it that he was the most likely candidate to take over as Auzraeria's Police Commissioner.

The Chief of Police simply nodded and waved goodbye to Officer Sullivan.

***

"Sir, the so-called bandits have all the papers and they can prove that the man is Frank, and since Belinda hasn't raised that doubt, we think that the 'brother' is either hallucinating or he's an imposter himself," one of the police officers in the police tent on site reported to Officer Sullivan.

"I need to talk to Frank, and then Belinda in that order," Officer Sullivan ordered.

"Yes, sir," rushed another police officer

from the tent to get "Frank."

After just about seven minutes, "Frank" was in the tent facing Officer Sullivan.

"Tell me, what liquor did you feed to your brother-in-law, mhm…what's happening?"

"Officer…?" 'Frank' wanted to know the officer's name and station.

"I am Grant Sullivan, Officer Sullivan, I am the Assistant Chief of Police Interrogation Unit…"

"Thank you for showing up, sir. My name is Frank, Frank Galando, and I am here to marry my sweetheart, Belinda. Everything was going well until Gavo began to go wild in his head…I heard that he's been undergoing some psychiatric evaluation or something…"

"End there, you said 'psychiatric evaluation'?"

"Yes, sir. When he just arrived from Docrberg, he was hospitalized for two days for some mental, you know…"

Officer Sullivan did not suspect anything ulterior from "Frank."

After "Frank" had left, Officer Sullivan did not want to wait to speak to Belinda.

"Change of plans. Call my good friend, Mukleff Tobius, he's the best in psychoanalytic conversations, and he can assist us to negotiate."

As one of the officers got into a police cruiser to look for the negotiator, one of the remaining police officers had something to report to Officer Sullivan.

"What is it, please go ahead and say it," Officer Sullivan gave the permission.

"Before your arrival here, sir, Gavo gave some conditions. When Frank wanted to get married so badly that he wanted Belinda to be rescued, Gavo imposed the following conditions: (1) That Frank shouldn't marry Belinda; (2) That Frank should leave Auzraeria;

and (3) That Frank must be investigated by the Farisian embassy in Auzraeria. Gavo doesn't think that Frank is Farisian; he believes that he is a thug from Auzraeria."

"Wow, this guy is truly mental…why would he claim that?"

One officer jumped in and spoke, "Sir, Gavo said that it was obvious that when the wedding was cancelled, 'Frank' wouldn't inherit Belinda's wealth. He also added that the only reason 'Frank' was here was because of Belinda's money…"

"How so?" Officer Sullivan probed.

"Yes, Sir. He also said that although 'Frank' staged himself as Frank, he was not a Farisian and if he were to go to Farisia, his scandalous behavior might be revealed and he would be imprisoned for life there…"

"What…this guy is truly a lunatic…"

"But, Sir, there is even more…"

"Go on, officer."

"He gave a rationale. He said that if we wanted to prove him right, we should ask 'Frank' to be interrogated by the Farisian Embassy in Auzraeria. He further…"

"What, officer, there is more?"

"Yes, Sir. And we thought of bringing this to your attention earlier but you were talking. Gavo's reasoning makes some sense when he claims that 'Frank' would refuse to be handed over to the Farisian Embassy…"

"Why do you think so, officers?' Officer Sullivan was becoming reasonable.

"Thank you, Sir. This is exactly what I wrote in my notes, 'Because he feared that if investigated, it would take just few hours before his real identity could be revealed.' Gavo reasoned that it would be better for the Farisian government to investigate 'Frank' than the Auzraerian government. Gavo feared that 'Frank' had leverage over the Auzraerian government and police and he also suspected him to influence peddle the outcome."

"But this is in our jurisdiction, isn't it?" Officer Sullivan asked.

"No, Sir, 'Frank' holds an international passport, *here* is a copy."

There was a long pause.
Then Officer Sullivan spoke.

"The condition of doing the three would result in Gavo letting Belinda go without marrying Frank; and Gavo would be handed over to the Farisian government for prosecution. Do I get it right?"

"What I think, Sir, is that this might need a good lawyer to review."

"I am beginning to believe so. Thank you, guys."

"You're welcome, Officer Sullivan," the officers all said it at the same time.

***

Mukleff Tobius was the negotiator.

"Listen, Frank, this is a good offer. If you love Belinda, you will agree, and who knows after the fracas, you two could come together. The issue here is Belinda's wellbeing," Mukleff advised.

"No, Mr. Tobius. This man is an extortionist. Who knows, if he was able to pretend to be Belinda's brother what else he would do," 'Frank' declined Gavo's conditions.

Then "Frank" gave a counteroffer.

"What I am proposing is that you find a sniper and kill *that* imposter."

"But we can't do that, sir. As you know, this case is all over the news now. The current government would not risk losing an election over some woman and her foreign boyfriend. This *is* an election year," Mukleff rebutted.

After protracted negotiations, "Frank" agreed to not marrying Belinda, "But I won't agree to the other two. I still have a valid Visa to be here, and I have nothing to hide before my government. They know me and my inventions. I have a clean record in Farisia."

***

"Frank" wanted very much to convince Belinda to open up to him on all her investments, especially how many properties she owned.

Meanwhile, his men were trying to steal her banking details and to know her password combination to her safe, which "Frank" had discovered when he spent a night in Belinda's multibedroom mansion.

"Guys, we may be caught between a rock and a hard place, we must take as much before we make our final escape," 'Frank' mandated his group of hoodlums.

Just as "Frank" was giving his command to the group, there was a knock on the quarter's door.

"It's Moffat. Madam wants to have a word with you, sir."

"I am coming, give me few seconds."

"Yes, sir."

"Who was that?" Mikoshev wanted to know.

"It's that chap who does the gardening; I'll be back."

When "Frank" approached Belinda, he could not believe for the first time in his life that he was afraid of a woman. He thought that she could see through him. He was so timid that he called her by the name of his deceased wife.

"Hello *Madea*, did you call me, I meant 'Belinda,'?" He asked, but Belinda did not even hear it as "Madea," she heard it as "my dear."

"I am fine, *Mr. Galando*, I heard that you were trying to cancel the marriage, are you giving up on *us*, then?"

"No, not really. I thought that…"

"What now, dear, I thought that you and I already know that my brother is not okay in his head, don't we?"

"Yes, indeed, and that's what I had said to Officer Sullivan, but…"

"But what, dear?"

"Well, the negotiator kept shifting the goalposts, so I thought that it could be in your best interest that we stop all these, what do you think?"

"*Me*, I don't think, I know that you're the one for me. Let's follow through to the end. We will go in there tomorrow as a team, you and I, do you hear me, Darling?" Belinda said.

"Okay, Partner, let's do so. I love you," 'Frank' hugged Belinda and gave her a light kiss on her lips.

8 | DISCOVERY

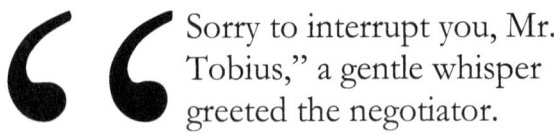Sorry to interrupt you, Mr. Tobius," a gentle whisper greeted the negotiator.

"And what is it, Doriah, you can see that I am in the middle of…"

"…an important negotiation, I get it… but a body has been discovered near the Marionkobell, sir."

"What does that have to do with this negotiation?"

Doriah pulled the chief negotiator aside and whispered something in his ear. And all of a sudden, the negotiator's face turned red.

"I...I ...must be excused...briefly...Mr. Cikaya..." The negotiator stammered.

And he did not wait for Gavo to respond. He just stormed out of the makeshift room they used as a detention center for Gavo.

Since they brought him there, Gavo had wondered why the police chose to believe 'Frank' and not him. But Gavo did not know that it was Belinda's idea.

"Officer," she had begun, "...my so-called brother has brought nothing but contempt. Since he came, there has been chaos here with his outrageous conduct..."

"...are you saying that..." Officer Sullivan, the assistant chief of police interrogation unit, was about to say something, but he, too, was interrupted.

"...I doubt if he even *is* my brother. Can you perform a DNA test, I have his hairbrush

with me in the house."

Following that conversation, DNA test was performed and the results were in. When Doriah disclosed to the negotiator the result, the negotiator had become pale.

His negotiation theory had been greatly altered. He was staking on the fact that DNA would prove that Gavo was not Belinda's brother which would be cause for continued detention according to *Auzraerian Penal Code.*

"It doesn't make sense…how can this poor fellow not be a scammer seeing that he's seen an opportunity to gain…" The negotiator was interrupted again, and again it was by Doriah.

"Sir, they have found a body!"

***

The body had no clothes on it but it bore no direct resemblance to Frank's face or features because it had no head and its right thumb was missing.

But investigations showed that the T.A was spotted around the same area they found the body. CCTV had captured a man who looked

like Frank's right hand man throwing the body.

Mikoshev was still under interrogation at the police headquarters. He had remained quiet for most of the time.

"You are saying that Mikoshev dumped the body?"

"Yes, sir…and…"

"And what, Doriah? Frank is now a suspect, that can't be…"

"I'm sure this development means…"

"That they can't continue to detain Gavo, I get it, Doriah."

"Yes, sir."

Unknown to Frank, Gavo's statement that he had stumbled upon the real Frank's laptop and had discovered a human finger in the T.A's freezer had begun to gain credibility.

9 | JUSTICE

"Order in Court, Judge George Fennington is presiding," Clerk Philip Metpot's bass voice rang in the open space like a meteorite.

The court structure itself was a makeshift tent erected at the Cikaya Ranch as Belinda's hacienda came to be known.

The Crown as the prosecution was called in Auzraeria was represented by Milory Mufwamba, a twenty-seven year veteran in criminal justice.

During arraignment a fortnight earlier, Milory had brought a motion under subsection 4.4 of the *Auzraerian Penal Code* to conduct a site trial because "one of our critical pieces of evidence is a motor vehicle, My Lord, Your Honor," he had argued.

Milory had become famous because of the book he wrote titled, *The Reclusive Suspect: Trial by Fire.*

The book had showcased the cross-examination of Moriati, Auzraeria's most intelligent criminal, who was never convicted of crimes he had committed. He always found a weakness in the prosecution's case and exploited it for his own advantage. The book had become a primer in university law schools across Auzraeria.

"The defence finds no relevance in conducting the trial off the courthouse grounds and we also deem it as a waste of the taxpayers money. In addition…" echoed Maybin Carson, a seasoned defence attorney, nicknamed, "The rich man' sachet."

He prided himself in representing celebrities and extremely wealthy clients.

"Objection, My Lord, Your Honor…" Milory stomped on his feet.

"Reason?" Judge Fennington asked, calmly.

"Inconvertible circumstances and the nature of the crime, the vehicle itself is a witness, My Lord…"

"Sustained," Judge Fennington did not even wait for the prosecution to rest their reasoning for the motion.

"But…" started Maybin, "…in *Rivers v. The People*…"

"…end right there, Counsel Carson…you wish to advance the controversial 'familiarity' argument…I have read the brief, except for one witness, namely, Ms. Belinda Cikaya, the rest of the witnesses are either unfamiliar with this ranch or are foreign to our country."

"I understand, My Lord, Your Honor," resigned Maybin.

That was how the trial came to be conducted at the Cikaya Ranch.

***

"How did I do, Mr. Mufwamba?" Belinda asked, after a spirited cross-examination from Maybin.

"I think fifty-fifty, Ms. Cikaya."

"You mean because I couldn't answer Frank's middle name and about his family, I saw how that *demon* laughed, mhm," Belinda sank into her seat, dejected.

"No need to worry much, that's expected of relationships that begin online, it's new territory, you know," Milory encouraged.

But everyone in the prosecution team, including the deputy lead investigator, Jennifer Brooms, who stood in for Officer Grant Sullivan who did not appear for the prosecution because of a family emergency, looked concerned.

The negotiator was precluded from testifying by the recent amendment made to the constitution.

"But I would have preferred Mr. Tobius to have testified, because other than you and your brother, he's the only outsider who spent some quality time with him," Crown Attorney, Milory, said.

And the mood was already somber when Gavo gave out a jot of disappointment in himself, "I couldn't think of the real Frank's clothes because I was in a hood; all I did there was thinking of my own survival first."

"Well, the defence had their day today, we can just hope that we find their weakness when 'Frank' takes the stand next week," Milory said, but his own demeanor betrayed his voice.

As the room in Belinda's huge Elizabethan mansion built by the mixture of mahogany and oak timber during the later 19th century, was quickly emptying, Belinda grabbed Milory's left hand before he exited the room and asked:

"What would happen if we lost, sir?"

"Not only the face, and, of course, the imposter gets to keep the real Frank's vehicle

and patent rights to it, why do you ask, ma'am?"

"Just in case, will I be forced to still marry him?"

"Mhm… only if you two so desire, I think… but that's more of a family law matter than criminal…you can…"

"…ask a family law lawyer, I understand… but…"

"Say it, ma'am, but what…" Milory said, so that he sounded polite and caring.

"If he's a criminal as my brother said, he already knows too much about me and everything *here*, I am afraid we'll be vulnerable to his revenge?" Belinda said it in a concerned way without giving the impression that she had already accepted defeat.

Milory did not say anything but he only parted Belinda on the back as a reassurance that the defence's case was still pending.

***

"Ohm…he whacked them clean, no wonder they call him a sachet for rich people…we are gonna be stinking rich when we acquire the vehicle, Boss," Mikoshev could not hide his excitement about the way the case was going for them.

Meanwhile, Mikoshev's own criminal case was pending. Bail pending trial had been posted in the amount of UAS$500,000.00 recognizance.

But unknown to Mikoshev, a warrant for his arrest was being drafted as the trial was going on. His fingerprint had revealed that he was Nicholaz Mikoshev who was wanted in the over-367 new charges in the Auzraecress Region. With that discovery, the fate of the Antiviap Cartel was in limbo.

"But you've cost me $50,000.00 in lawyer fees, which I could have kept for myself. Now we have only $250,000.00 of the cash we found in his T.A," the Boss was angry at Mikoshev's carelessness in disposing of Frank's body, and the subsequent arrest and release on bail.

"I agree with the Boss. I had suggested that we dump the decapitated body in a river but *you* refused and now look…"

"D," as they called him did not even finish talking when he received a slap on the face from Mikoshev.

"D" responded with a slap of his own to Mikoshev's defenseless back. And there was commotion inside the servants quarters of the hacienda where they were staying.

"Stop! Everyone, stop, I am trying to think out here. Although we're winning, I am yet to figure out how to maneuver this vehicle thing and if we'll not show up somewhere as the Antiviap Cartel…"

The place went quiet.

Muravi, the group's computer geek, had a report to give.

"I cracked the electronic diary. Boss, remember his real name is 'Frank Kuliano Mantosha,' just as it is in his passport. But here the diary puts it even better:

'Frank Kuliano Mantosha, one of the two surviving sons of Mary Morris Mantosha and Frank Everland Kuliano Mantosha.'

So, Boss, surprise them with this. Remember, Belinda failed to state his full name…at trial…"

"Yeah, of course, because owing to my brilliance, I have not shown her this passport…"

The entire team of seven, including their boss, burst into shouts of "Aye, aye, aye," toasting glasses of gin and vodka around them.

When they rested from cheers, Muravi broke the silence.

"On a serious note, Team, I am concerned about this vehicle, I read somewhere in the manual that it can talk…" Muravi said, but his sentiments were impugned as senseless.

"Where on earth did you hear of a car talking, does it have flesh and blood?" 'Frank' mocked.

"This is not in the Bible where a donkey spoke, and at least, an animal has a mouth," Mikoshev was all over Muravi.

As the group laughed, Sharon, the only female member of the group and who was also responsible for finances interrupted.

"I have heard of AI, do you think that Mura might be sensible?"

"What's AI?" Mikoshev asked, but it looked like no-one was even listening to him.

Then Drew Fo chimed in and made a familiar comment.

"*Nunu*, you're smarter than Mura by my judgment, how on earth would you think this piece of metal can talk, and even if it did…"

Drew Fo was interrupted by their boss,' "…yes, and so what if it did?"

"Boss, you have heard of computer programming, 'garbage in garbage out,' haven't you?"

"Of course, it can only bring out what is in there…" Mikoshev was in mid-sentence when Muravi agreed with him, unexpectedly.

"…and thanks, *Dicer*, Boss, there's no cause to worry."

But Mikoshev was enraged to be addressed by his epithet, which he loathed because it had almost made him get killed. Five years before he had drilled a competitor gang member with a driller (for so they called a nail-hammering machine) when the Boss' instructions were "not to mess with his brain."

The boss had wanted to retrieve as much information as possible from the victim before he died. The boss, however, would save Mikoshev if he spent one week without going to the toilet to either pee or poop.

When the seventh day came, Mikoshev had failed to hold, and he smelled like freshly crashed skunk from the poop and pee that saddled his pants and underwear, thus, earning the nickname, "Dicer."

***

"You've always said, 'Do no harm,' after such a self-incriminating testimony by the prosecution main witness, Belinda. So, it's my hope that you will do little or less to disturb the flow, sir," Beverley Msizoskos advised her own boss, Maybin, before they entered the courtroom tent to continue the trial.

Msoz is right. The prosecution have done nothing or less to advance their case. I must consider calling or not calling Mulinger Haggard, the so-called "Frank" to take the witness stand, Maybin thought.

The light came up into the tent and the prosecution and the defence had already started gathering.

"*Msoz, I need to talk to Mr. Haggard before we enter the courtroom, call him, please*," Maybin whispered.

"Sure, Boss, right away."

"Frank" and his entourage had already entered the tent when Maybin and Msizoskos reached the tent. The judge had not arrived yet. So, Msizoskos approached "Frank" and whispered in his ear, "Sir, Mr. Carson would

like to have a word with you before trial restarts; he's waiting for you in the lobby."

"Frank" was very offended and he retorted, "Girl, who is paying who here? I pay him well so he can serve me. If it's so important then let him come to me."

All those seated around "Frank" heard him. The group members heaped insults on Msizoskos. She retreated embarrassingly and reported to the defence attorney.

"Okay, I will go to him," Maybin said, and within less than a minute he was kneeling beside his client.

"What is it that's so urgent that you decided to disturb my peace, Maybin, mhm?"

"There has been some development. The Crown now wants you to testify, sir."

"Didn't you tell me that it was okay not to testify, that I can even plead the fifth?"

"Well, that was the idea until…"

"Until what, now?"

"You see, the Crown brought a motion and we just finished, it was heard in chambers. Sorry, it was so urgent that I couldn't inform you."

"Maybin, what happened?"

"We…it …they decided that you must testify…"

"How come, aren't you the lawyer who works miracles?"

"A lawyer I am, miracles I don't think it's in my CV, however, I can ask the Court to adjourn this case to tomorrow to have you prepare for it?"

"Was that meant to be a question or request?" 'Frank' asked.

"It's my advice, sir, you hired me to provide legal advice."

"No, Maybin, I am ready to go. What can they ask me that I can't answer…"

"… but sir…there's a risk…"

"…what is it Maybin?"

"You can't bring up new issues other than what the prosecution have already stated… moreover…"

"…moreover what, you lawyers!" 'Frank' pointed a vindictive right index finger at his lawyer.

"Sorry about that, sir. I meant no offence. It's only that until recently before the *Code* was amended, you could refuse to answer certain questions, but now it enables the judge to adduce a negative inference if you refuse to answer."

"Wow, Maybin, I paid you to represent me but now you're teaching me criminal law?"

"No, sir, that's why I suggested that we adjourn for a day to allow you and me to discuss strategy."

"No, our strategy is straightforward, to

prove that I am the real Frank and that Gavo is a lunatic, do you hear me?"

"Sure, sure, sir. But...you should know that the police found another body…"

"What are you talking about, Maybin?"

"A body showed up near the Kingpeng Airstrip. Investigations are under way, but already they are pointing finger at your team, sir."

"Is that so?" 'Frank' asked in a rather dejected voice. He was about to ask more questions when there was a clerks' call to order.

"Silence in Court, Judge Fennington is presiding."

10 | SPOILER

The weather was what in Kingpeng they considered to be superb, neither too hot nor too cold. It was just perfect. There had been a few rains drops in the early hours of that morning, but by 2.00 p.m., the temperature hovered in around 33°C or 91.4°F.

Before its independence from the United American States (UAS), the standard unit of temperature measurement was the Fahrenheit. But upon obtaining self-rule, some 90 years ago, it had adopted the degree Celsius.

Due to the reforms brought about by the Labor Party of Auzraeria (LPA), judges were no longer required to wear their judge's robes when presiding. Any suite would do as long as it was black, brown, navy blue or dark grey.

Judge George Fennington was wearing his signature navy blue suite with a black necktie and black shoes. He was a lanky sixty-six year old man who had relished the idea of "old school" regime in which judges were referred to as "Your Lordship."

With the LPA reforms, lawyers and those appearing before the courts of justice could choose to refer to judges as "Mr.," "Madam," or simply as "Mr. or Madam Judge." However, those who were old school still preferred to address judges formerly as "My Lordship, Your Honor."

Judge George Fennington preferred the old school model and had instructed, when asked how he would like to be address, "Please, address me as 'My Lordship, Your Honor.'"

"The defence would like to call its first and only witness, Frank Kuliano Mantosha…"

"What, so he even has a middle name?" Belinda jumped from her seat in disgust.

"Order in Court!" Judge Fennington ordered while simultaneously hammering his gavel hard on his table.

"I am sorry, Sir," Belinda sat down, still expressing disgust on her face.

"Mr. Carson, you may continue…proceed…" ordered the judge, without even paying attention to Belinda's apology.

Seated closer to his lawyer, and just before he sat up to enter the witness box, "Frank" smiled and whispered to his lawyer, "Even the judge doesn't like her."

But Maybin Carson was focused on his task at hand and he did not mind his client's comments.

"Yes, we are ready, My Lordship, Your Honor…" Maybin instructed his client to hasten to sit in the witness box using his left

hand signal.

"Frank" stretched himself out, revealing his biceps and well-ripped and chiseled chest. He wore a slim fit and tightly held grey suite with a silvery blue shirt but without a necktie or bowtie on it. His hair was well kempt and he wore an expensive Dor male perfume. At five-foot-nine he stood like a tower on display, drawing everyone's attention, including Belinda.

"Wow," Belinda said, and whether she was referring to his well-built muscular body or to his hypocrisy, no-one knew.

"State your full name for the record," Maybin prompted.

"Frank" staired in the roof, he was trying to remember the order as it was written in Frank's electronic diary. He seemed to have forgotten. He looked towards Muravi and Muravi did the trick. He mimed the start and "Frank" remembered.

"Sure, I will, proudly…" 'Frank' said.

"Please go ahead, His Lordship, is waiting.

"My name is Frank Kuliano Mantosha, one of the two surviving sons of Mary Morris Mantosha and Frank Everland Kuliano Mantosha."

At first, there was a rumbling sound as if mechanical actions where reforming themselves. Everyone was puzzled.

"Where is that noise coming from?" Some were asking.

"It's from the vehicle," another answered.

Then the T.A began talking.

Welcome, sir, although I sense that something wrong happened to the real you. You are fake. You are not Mr. Frank Kuliano Mantosha, one of the two surviving sons of Mary Morris Mantosha and Frank Everland Kuliano Mantosha.

"Stop that thing!" 'Frank' shouted, directing the command to Muravi.

"Order in Court!" Judge Fennington shouted on top of his voice.

Don't order me. You are not Mr. Frank Kuliano Mantosha, one of the two surviving sons of Mary Morris Mantosha and Frank Everland Kuliano Mantosha, the T.A repeated.

Frustrated, "Frank" left the witness box and went to the vehicle and shook it, hitting it hard to stop it.

"Stop talking!" 'Frank' shouted.

I will not stop. You are not Mr. Frank Kuliano Mantosha, one of the two surviving sons of Mary Morris Mantosha and Frank Everland Kuliano Mantosha, the T.A repeated itself.

Seeing that the T.A had become uncontrollable, Muravi sneaked out and ran. Then it was Mikoshev. He ran away.

When Maybin saw what was happening, to protect himself from ethical violations, he shouted, "Arrest Mulinger Haggard…that is his real name, *Your Lordship, My Honor*," messing up the order prescribed by Judge

Fennington.

Everyone got the idea. The judge stood and gave the order to the standing policemen, "Arrest 'Frank'!"

The four police officers began to run towards Mulinger Haggard.

Drew Fo, "D" and Sharon were trying to start the T.A so that they could scoop up their boss who was running on foot towards the thicket on the southwestern side of the ranch.

"'D,' bring the head and finger in the freezer, quickly," Drew Fo said.

"D" handed the human parts to Drew Fo, but the engine could not start. Rather another repeated voice from the T.A kept saying, *Engine disabled. You are not Mr. Frank Kuliano Mantosha, one of the two surviving sons of Mary Morris Mantosha and Frank Everland Kuliano Mantosha.*

Meanwhile, all that Drew Fo and "D" saw was Sharon coming inside the T.A holding her hands up and moving extremely slowly. Then

shortly after, everyone in the T.A knew what was happening. A policeman had pointed a gun at Sharon. The trio was arrested.

The other three police officers had continued to chase Mulinger Haggard and Muravi.

Mikoshev had disappeared in thin air.

However, a less known member of the seven, was gunned down by the police when he was running. Honda Haggard, the police later found out his true identity, was Mulinger Haggard's only son and the youngest member of the Antiviap Cartel, as the group of seven came to be revealed.

After just about less than 30 minutes, Muravi was arrested and brought to the ranch by one of the four police officers.

***

He had been running nonstop for close to seven hours. He was exhausted. He stopped near a ranch owned by the former vice president of the Republic of Auzraeria,

Thompson Musipee.

I must switch off my cellphone, he thought, *they could be tracking me*.

As he was about to turn the phone off, a news flash almost blinded his vision, "Honda Haggard, the son of the fugitive, Mulinger, is dead…" it hit him so hard that he shed a tear.

"Oh, Honda, Honda, my son, what have I done to you!" He moaned.

Then he made a promise to himself, "I will kill them. I will kill them all beginning with Gravo, Belinda, that judge…I will murder innocent civilians…I will kill them all…beginning with whoever is in *that* mansion…."

He hastened to go into the house. But first he must inspect if the fence was electric.
It was not.

"*Here…there…*" Mulinger Haggard pointed his right index finger to an opening on the fence. The opening might have been made by wolves which prowled those lands looking for

meat.

And it was getting late.

Soon these deadly carnivores will be roaming around the area, he thought.

He squeezed himself flat under the wires, he felt a stinging pain.

It's just nothing, he thought, reassuring himself.

Later when he was inside the ranch, he felt a tingling sensation, and then saw two bluish-purple bite marks on his left shoulder. It momentarily sent in a paralyzingly sharp and painful shock. He dropped to the ground.

It could be just a bite from a starving rat, he thought, trying to convince himself.

But as he moved forward towards a flicker of light in the distance, he could feel that strength was draining fast from his veins. In his mind, he was running at a faster speed, but his limbs were giving up.

"W-h-a-t…i-s…h-a-p-p-e-n-i-ng…t-o…m-e…" he was fast losing control.

He struggled to lift his jaws. But he was determined to reach the house.

He fell to the ground once and then he staggered up to his feet and knocked on the door.

Then he fainted.

"It's *him*, Mary," eighty-two year-old former vice president confirmed to his sixty-year-old wife.

He was vice president then when he divorced his childhood sweetheart and first wife, Gweyn, and married a famous actress and model, Mary Manford, a woman the same age as his first child, Brianna Musipee.

It was a controversial marriage then. But looking at it in retrospect, he sighed once and thought to himself, *As old age begins to pummel me, I am realizing that marrying Mary was the best decision of my entire life…she has practically been my limbs and eyes.*

"Yes, the same guy on news this evening. He's not lucky, though. He ran away from

regal justice but divine justice caught up with him. He's been beaten by a black mamba. He's got only three hours at most to live," Mary said, as she administered some antibiotics to cushion Mulinger's boiling heartbeats.

Then the fugitive woke up, albeit briefly. He was not tied up. He saw an old man speaking on phone and a woman bringing a basin of water.

Then he fainted, again.

It took exactly four hours from the time Mulinger dropped himself at their doorsteps, to the time they tried to resuscitate him, to when they called 911 and to the time they took him to the hospital.

Then, there was breaking news.

"Tom!" Mary called out to her husband who was in another room.

"Yes, dear, I am coming."

"He died."

"Who died, my dear?" He asked.

He did not need to hear the response from his wife, the television answered for him.

> *He has done it again. Former vice president, Mr. Thompson Musipee, has done it again. Over 30 years ago, he sponsored the controversial assisted dying legislation which became law and now he handed Auzraeria's most dangerous gang criminal to police on a silver platter. Bongoto General Hospital just announced that the notorious killer of 1000 just died a few minutes ago…and with his death, the end of the Antiviap Cartel!*

"You're again their hero, Tom," Mary said, jealously.

"Wait until I clarify it to them in the morning that *you're* the true hero here. You found him and tried to make him live."

The couple laughed.

"Darling, you are awake," Belinda Mantosha said.

"Mhm…Sweetheart, I was having a good dream and you just spoiled it like that."

"Really, I don't believe you, if it's true tell me, or tell *us* what it was all about," Belinda pointed to her five-month old baby bump.

"Okay, are you two ready?"

"On behalf of Belinda Junior, yes, we are."

"Sweetheart, we both know that it's a boy, so, Frank, the real Frank Junior."

"Oh, no. You're wrong, it's a girl and you know it," Belinda continued to feign being difficult when inside her heart she was overwhelmed with joy.

She remembered the ordeal. And she had a scar on her neck to show for it. He had hidden

himself inside her walk-in closet. When the police returned chasing after his boss and couldn't catch him, they turned their attention looking for him on the ranch. The judge had spoken to the Chief of Police to increase security on the Cikaya Ranch.

News on TV had broken and the names and faces of all the members of the Antiviap Cartel had been revealed. There was nowhere for Mikoshev to go.

Belinda had just gone to bed around 11:01 p.m. when she felt the sting of a kitchen knife caressing her beautiful long neck. She tried to get it off, but her delicate five-foot-five body could not hold the pressure.

No wander Boss went coocoo on her, Mikoshev thought, "…I wonder how these tiny legs are able to hold such large bums and these huge boobs," Mikoshev vocalized what was in his heart.

"You're hurting me," Belinda had cried, albeit in soft groans.

"You're my prisoner. We escape together

or die together."

But the night was not going to end well for Mikoshev. Gavo needed to have a word with her sister concerning the distrust that had developed between them due to the fake Frank's deception.

He came closer but the door was locked.

"Since I came to the hacienda Sis never locks the door. Could it be that she's afraid of the uncaught perpetrators," Gavo reasoned to himself.

When he knocked on her door, there was a hesitance then a faintly voice came through the door's lentil, "I am now asleep, Gavo. Let's chat tomorrow."

She's never called me by my name ever since I came, even when things were sour between us. Why calling me "Brother" now, and how did she know that it was me? Gavo thought.

But it was his quick thinking street smartness that saved his sister.

"Alright, Sis, sleep tight, chat tomorrow, bye," Gavo said.

When he reached the kitchen, Gavo inspected everything.

"*Nye, come over here*," Gavo whispered while tiptoeing towards the kitchen.

"What is it, sir," Nye, a thirty-seven-year old female in-house maidservant asked.

While still tiptoeing and putting his right middle finger on his mouth, he asked her, "Has this kitchen knife gone missing?"

"No, sir, all the knives must be here."

"Okay, go back to your room and lock it."

"Okay, sir," Nye said.

Gavo had alerted the policemen outside the house and together they came up with a plan that confirmed that Belinda was being held at gunpoint.

They had placed an amplifying device on

the door to Belinda's room and within minutes they had a hit. They heard Mikoshev instructing Belinda to put on her clothes because they were going to the garage to get a car and drive off.

"You'll tell the officers outside your house that you had a headache and you were going to buy painkillers. They'll believe after all that you've gone through in the day."

"Sure, I'll do that but if you answer one question," Belinda had offered.

"Lady, you are in no position to ask questions, you're my captive but I'll allow you only one question."

"Thank you…" Belinda started, "Did you kill Frank, the real Frank?"

"Of course, yes and it was me who chopped his head and thumb off…"

Belinda had begun to sob after hearing what Mikoshev revealed.

"Quickly, let's go!"

And no sooner had Mikoshev opened Belinda's door than a gun was pointed at him. Mikoshev surrendered and Belinda was rescued.

***

"I waited, Darling?" Belinda pressed.

"For what, Sweetheart?"

"For you to explain the dream to me."

"Oh, about that…I, indeed, saw a man confined in a room, chained to a bed and left with only two loaves of bread and a 30 liter container of water.

"A big bucket was left for him where to urinate and defecate. He was left in that condition for close to one month. He was literally looking at his shit heap upon heap until it started to flood the space. After about ten days, he couldn't distinguish the smell of faeces from the bread that he lived on.

"Meanwhile, his T.A, bank book, passport

and about $280,000.00 in cash were taken.

"On the twentieth or thirteenth day, he passed out and woke up on intravenous (IV) treatment to be resuscitated.

"His own brother had done so. Fortunately, or unfortunately, he learned that his brother had been unlucky, running into thugs who decapitated his head and thumb. After taking his brother's T.A, he had reconfigured the Artificial Intelligence engineered motor vehicle to his own face and thumb recognition system but…"

"But what, Darling, keep talking?" Belinda encouraged Frank who was at that point sobbing profusely.

"Two weeks before he took his brother's T.A, money and documents, Brian, had come to me, begging me to volunteer unspecified amounts of time to learn about the AI powered technology. I didn't suspect anything, so I allowed him. He worked many hours in my workshop until …"

Frank stopped talking.

"Darling, why have you stopped talking…?"

"Some water, please," Frank asked.

"Sure, drink my love, drink… and you told me that during his internship at Tickfogree Aeromatic Inc., the company that you founded and that built the T.A motor vehicle, he observed how you were absorbed into me on social media and on the dating apps…"

"Right…" Frank agreed.

Belinda continued highlighting what Frank had told her when he was released from hospital.

"That, one day in a joking way, Brian Morris Mantosha, your brother, mentioned that I was his type when he saw a photo of me on your kitchen fridge…"

"You're right…"

"That you didn't think much about it, Brian being your brother, and you took it as

banter…"

"Right… in fact, I felt truly great, like a vote of confidence in my type of choice…"

"But, of course, Brian had an ulterior motive and other plans…"

"Yes, remember I told you that once he took the T.A for an entire day and when he returned it the other day, the remote sensor had been broken or disabled…" Frank wanted Belinda not to forget that part.

"But after he kidnapped you and stole from you that's when you realized that he had changed the self-recognized features of the T.A to fit his own tastes and…"

There was a knock on the door. It was Nye.

"Ma'am, the massage therapist is here for the daily morning session."

"I am coming…" Belinda told Nye, then she turned to Frank and said, "Gavo has that sixth sense; he warned me about that thug but I ignored him. When he returns from

Docrberg, please give him a foreman position at T.A. Inc…"

Belinda and Frank laughed.

"I know that look…you're thinking he'll swindle me the…" Belinda paused.

"…way Brian did…" Frank completed.

"No way, besides my brother, Gavo, is not gay, he just pretends to be one."

"Are you sure?" Frank teased."